The National Constitution Center

Giant walk–through heart at the Franklin Institute

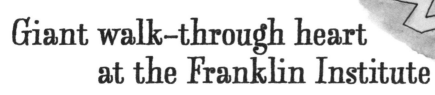

Elfreth's Alley

ON THE LOOSE
IN PHILADELPHIA

Dear Animal Detectives,

The animals included in this book are ones I thought you would recognize and have fun finding (at least in these pages) on the streets of Philadelphia. Many of them can be found at the Philadelphia Zoo. Because the zoo is constantly moving animals to other zoos around the country and bringing in new animals from countries around the globe, it's always exciting to find out what animals the zoo has at any given time. The Philadelphia Zoo currently houses more than 1,300 animals, including many species that are rare or endangered. For more information, visit http://www.philadelphiazoo.org. Or, better yet, visit the zoo in person.

P.S. In real life the zoo does an excellent job making sure its animals are very happy at home and don't go wandering off!

ON THE LOOSE
IN PHILADELPHIA

A Find-the-Animals Book

Written and Illustrated
by Sage Stossel

Commonwealth Editions
Carlisle, Massachusetts

For Mike and Kieran

ISBN 978-1-938700-15-6

Series design by John Barnett/4 Eyes Design

Commonwealth Editions is an imprint of Applewood Books Inc.,
Carlisle, Massachusetts 01741
Visit us on the web at www.commonwealtheditions.com

Visit Sage Stossel on the web at www.sagestossel.com

Printed in China

10 9 8 7 6 5 4

In the city of Philly,
in famed Fairmount Park,
lies our land's oldest zoo,
which closes at dark.

One morning the keeper
discovered a note:
"We've gone for a walk,"
the animals wrote.

"Oh, dear," said the keeper,
"what am I to do?
My critters have left me
alone at the zoo!"

The cages indeed were all empty that day,
for the creatures, it seemed, had meandered away.

1 leopard, 1 penguin, 1 aardvark, 1 alligator, 1 hippo, 1 brown bear, 2 snakes,
1 lion, 1 rhino, 1 flamingo, 1 camel, 3 monkeys, 2 lemurs, and 1 turtle?

CAN YOU FIND

Then from down in Old City there came a quick call:
"A camel's cavorting at Independence Hall!"

1 camel, 2 monkeys, 1 aardvark, 2 antelopes, 1 kangaroo, 1 snake, 1 penguin, 2 lemurs, 1 flamingo, 1 giraffe, 1 emu, 2 rhinos, 1 brown bear, 1 alligator, and 1 lion?

CAN YOU FIND

Things next got a bit rowdy at Rittenhouse Square,
where a mischievous monkey did flips through the air.

3 monkeys, 1 polar bear, 1 peacock, 2 lemurs, 2 snakes, 2 rhinos, 1 alligator, 1 tiger, 1 penguin, 1 emu,
1 giraffe, 1 turtle, 1 kangaroo, and 1 aardvark? (Do you also see a bronze statue of a lion?)

CAN YOU FIND

The quiet on Quince Street was shattered as well,
when a baby was bumped by a grazing gazelle.

1 gazelle, 2 penguins, 1 tiger, 1 lemur, 1 turtle, 1 camel, 1 hippo, 1 snake, 1 aardvark, 1 kangaroo, 1 monkey, 1 rhino, and 1 lion?

CAN YOU FIND

At the Seaport Museum, the crowds were astir,
as tourists rubbed shoulders with critters with fur.

1 tiger, 1 polar bear, 1 rhino, 1 camel, 1 monkey, 1 emu, 1 penguin, 1 flamingo, 1 lion, 1 lemur, 1 snake, 1 brown bear, 1 kangaroo, 1 alligator, and 1 hippo?

CAN YOU FIND

Shoppers on 9th Street said, "Isn't that cute?"
when a ravenous rhino devoured some fruit.

2 rhinos, 1 alligator, 1 turtle, 2 monkeys, 1 kangaroo, 1 giraffe, 1 tiger, 1 snake, 1 emu, 1 flamingo, 2 brown bears, and 1 lemur?

CAN YOU FIND

True fans of the Phillies did happy high-fives
when an outfielding otter chased down some line drives.

1 otter, 2 hippos, 1 antelope, 1 giraffe, 1 tiger, 1 monkey, 1 emu, 1 lion, 1 lemur, 2 brown bears, 1 kangaroo, 1 rhino, 1 snake, 1 alligator, and 1 camel?

CAN YOU FIND

At the grand art museum, folks stood on their toes
to see kangaroos strike a "Rocky"-like pose.

3 kangaroos, 1 emu, 2 snakes, 2 lions, 1 monkey, 2 lemurs, 1 alligator, 1 penguin, 1 camel, 2 giraffes, 1 antelope, 1 rhino, 1 polar bear, 1 turtle, and 1 tiger?

CAN YOU FIND

At the curbside cafés, where trendsetters dine,
some patrons were joined by the nonhuman kind.

1 rhino, 1 monkey, 1 brown bear, 2 penguins, 1 flamingo, 2 lemurs, 1 lion, 1 aardvark, 1 snake, 1 antelope, 1 alligator, 1 tiger, and 1 parrot?

CAN YOU FIND

Down by the river, along Boathouse Row,
a red river hog raced his boat to and fro.

1 red river hog, 1 camel, 1 monkey, 1 emu, 1 rhino, 1 alligator, 2 hippos, 2 giraffes, 1 penguin, 1 aardvark, 2 kangaroos, 1 lion, 1 brown bear, and 1 turtle?

CAN YOU FIND

At JFK Plaza, a snake smooched a dove,
inspired, perhaps, by the statue of Love?

2 snakes, 1 dove, 2 turtles, 1 lemur, 1 brown bear, 1 emu, 1 antelope, 1 camel, 2 rhinos, 1 lion, 1 tiger, 1 aardvark, 1 penguin, 1 hippo, and 1 kangaroo?

CAN YOU FIND

When at last night descended,
the zookeeper smiled,
as back through the gate
all his animals filed.

What a wonderful day
they appeared to have had,
but to be back at home
they seemed equally glad.

As for where they had been,
they refused to confess,
but the keeper was smart
and could probably guess.

SAGE STOSSEL is a contributing editor for the *Atlantic* and a cartoonist for the *Boston Globe*, theatlantic.com, the *Provincetown Banner* (for which she received a New England Press Association Award), and other publications. Her cartoons have been featured by the *New York Times Week in Review*, *CNN Headline News*, Best Editorial Cartoons of the Year, and other venues. Her graphic novel, *Starling*, was published in 2013. Other books by Sage Stossel in the "On the Loose" series include *On the Loose in Boston* and *On the Loose in Washington, D.C.*

Visit onthelooseinphiladelphia.com for Philadelphia pictures to print and color, ideas for things to do around the city, and more.

Please Touch Museum

MEMORIAL HALL
FAIRMOUNT PARK

Rocky
Statue
at the
Philadelphia
Museum
of Art

Geno's
Steaks